Henrietta's Fourth of July

Henrietta's Fourth of July

By Syd Hoff

GARRARD PUBLISHING COMPANY
CHAMPAIGN, ILLINOIS

JE
c. 4

Library of Congress Cataloging in Publication Data

Hoff, Syd, 1912-
    Henrietta's Fourth of July.

    (An Imagination book)
    Summary: Farmer Gray and the barnyard friends,
including Henrietta, join in the annual Fourth of July
festivities.
        [1. Fourth of July — Fiction.   2. Domestic animals —
Fiction.]   I. Title.   II. Series: Imagination book.
PZ7.H672Hde   [E]   81-2334
ISBN 0-8116-4422-7   AACR2

Henrietta's Fourth of July

It was early in the morning.
Mr. Gray put up the flag.
"Today is the Fourth of July,"
he said.
"Will there be a parade?"
asked Henrietta.

"Yes, and I will march in it,"
said Mr. Gray.

He marched around the farm.
"Left-right, left-right,"
said Mr. Gray.

Henrietta followed him.
"Left-right, left-right,"
said Henrietta.

Then Henrietta stopped.
"Marching is fun.
May all the animals
march in the parade?"
she asked.

"If they want to,"
Mr. Gray told her.

Henrietta ran
to ask the animals.

"Would you like to march
in the Fourth of July parade?"
she said.

"That would be fun,"
said Winthrop the pig.
"I'd like that,"
said Patrick the goat.

"We all want
to be in the parade,"
said the chickens, cows,
geese, ducks, and horses.
"Let's go!"

They marched
to Mr. Gray's house.
"Left-right, left-right,"
said Henrietta.

Mr. Gray was waiting.
"Henrietta,
you may carry the flag,"
he said.

"What can we do?"
asked Winthrop and Patrick.

"I know,"

said Mr. Gray.

He went into the house.

"Winthrop can play this fife,
and Patrick can beat the drum,"
Mr. Gray said.

The animals got into the truck.
On the way into town,
Henrietta held the flag.
Winthrop blew on the fife.
Patrick beat the drum.

Henrietta sang.

"Yankee Doodle
went to town,
riding on a pony,
Stuck a feather
in his hat
and called it Macaroni."

The Fourth of July parade
had just started.
A tall man in a high hat
led the parade.

"Hooray for Uncle Sam!"
shouted the children.

"Here comes the band,"
said the people.

OOOMPAH! OOMPAH!

went the trombones and tubas.

BOOM! BOOM! BOOM!

went the drums.

The parade was a long one.

There were young people in it.

There were old people in it.

"Oh, here comes Henrietta.
The animals are with her,"
shouted the children.

The animals marched
in straight lines.
"Left-right, left-right,"
called Mr. Gray.

"Yankee Doodle
went to town,
riding on a pony,"
sang Henrietta.

"Marching is fun,
but my feet hurt,"
said a goose.
"Mine hurt too,"
said a duck.

"The parade is almost over,"
Henrietta told the animals.

"When will we eat?"
asked Winthrop.
"I'm hungry."

"We will eat now,"
said Mr. Gray.

There was a good picnic
for everyone.
There was food
for the animals.

Everyone ate and ate.

Soon it was dark.
"The fireworks are next,"
said Henrietta.
"They are the best part
of the Fourth of July."

BANG! BANG! BANG!

went the firecrackers.

SWISH! SWISH! BOOM!
went the skyrockets.

"There's a picture
of Uncle Sam,"
said Mr. Gray.

The animals watched the fireworks.
They saw one picture after another.

"The fireworks are beautiful,"
they said.

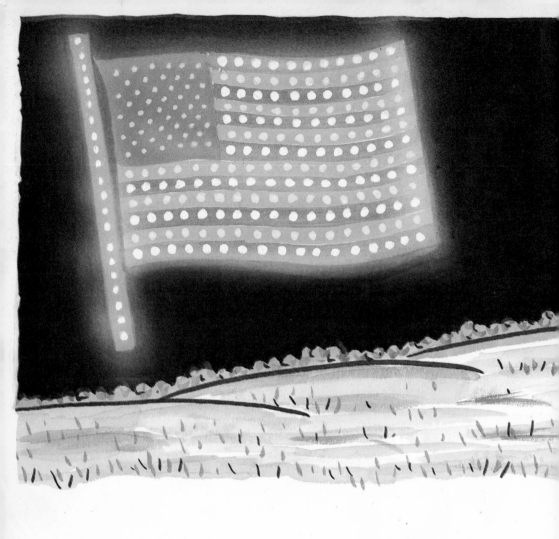

BANG!
The last one
was a picture of the flag.

"Hooray, hooray
for the red, white, and blue!"
shouted Henrietta.

"Now it's time to go home,"
said Mr. Gray.

The animals
rode back to the farm.
They were tired but happy.

"It was a good Fourth of July,"
said Winthrop.

"It was the best day we ever had,"
said Patrick.

Henrietta still held the flag.
"I wish every day
could be the Fourth of July,"
she said.